This edition published by Parragon Books Ltd in 2014

Parragon Books Ltd
Chartist House
15–17 Trim Street
Bath BA1 1HA, UK
www.parragon.com

ISBN 978-1-4723-7258-1

Printed in China

On his journey, Pooh passed by his friend Eeyore's house.

"I can't help noticing," said Pooh, "that you seem slightly gloomier than usual."

"Eeyore," said Pooh as he circled around him. "What has happened to your tail?"

"What has happened to it?" Eeyore wondered.

"Well, it isn't there," Pooh told him.

"That explains everything," said Eeyore sadly.

Eeyore's friends decided to hold a contest to find the donkey a new tail. The prize would be a lovely pot of golden honey.

Pooh gave Eeyore a Pooh-koo clock, hoping it would be the winning tail – but Eeyore accidentally broke it.

The friends tried a great many more things for Eeyore's tail – and a great many more things after that.

None of them worked.

"It's okay," said Eeyore sadly. "I'll learn to live without it."

A little while later, Pooh stopped by Christopher Robin's house looking for honey. Instead, he found a note. Pooh brought it to Owl.

"It says," began Owl, "'gone out, busy Backson.'" He looked horrified. "Our dear friend Christopher Robin has been captured by a creature called the Backson! It's malicious, ferocious and worst of all... terribly busy!"

Owl added that Backsons scribbled in library books, stopped clocks and put holes in socks. The more the friends learned, the more terrified they became!

But then Rabbit came up with a clever plan. They would collect things that the Backson liked, and leave a trail of them to lure him into a pit. Then the Backson would be trapped – and they could get Christopher Robin back!

While their friends went to gather the items that were needed, Pooh and Piglet got straight to work on the pit. Piglet disguised the trap as a lovely picnic, complete with a honeypot.

"Well, it certainly fooled me and my tummy," admitted Pooh.

Tigger, meanwhile, had decided to track
the Backson on his own. He was surprised
to come upon Eeyore, who had somehow
gotten left behind by the others.
    "You and me are going to catch
that Backson together!" Tigger promised.
"We just need to get you tiggerized!"

Tigger started with the
easy part: giving Eeyore stripes.
Teaching him to bounce was
another matter!
    The donkey bounced up
and down, up and down, and
finally, just up!

Eventually, the friends ended up in Rabbit's garden. Tigger dressed up as the Backson, and tried to show Eeyore how to "bounce" the monster. The poor donkey ricocheted all over the place before landing in the woods beyond. He hoped Tigger wouldn't find him. Being a tigger was exhausting!

In another part of the Wood, Pooh, Piglet and the rest of the friends were laying the trail of items.

RUMBLE! went Pooh's tummy, unhappy that honey had yet to come its way that day. Pooh did his best to ignore it.

Then something very strange happened....

Pooh's shadow stopped looking like a Pooh Bear, and started
looking like a honeypot! Next the flowers and trees – and even the
ground beneath Pooh's feet – melted into a giant wave of honey!
He rode the wave to a honey beach where he swam beneath a honey
ocean. Pooh was so blissfully happy that he sang a honey song and
danced a honey dance. Life was sweet!

POOF! Pooh's beautiful daydream suddenly disappeared. His honey ocean was really a muddy puddle! Pooh cleaned himself off and went on his way.

After a few steps, he came upon a picnic, complete with a honeypot! Pooh ran to the pot – and immediately fell into the pit that he and Piglet had dug earlier that day! The honeypot wedged itself tightly on his head. Unfortunately for Pooh and his tummy, it was empty.

Meanwhile, Pooh's friends had arrived back at the pit and were looking everywhere for him. Then, all at once, they heard a loud **THUD!**

"The plan worked!" Rabbit exclaimed. "We caught the Backson!"

The friends clung to each other in fear.

"Alright Backson," said Rabbit as the group peered into the pit. "Give us Christopher Robin back."

"Oh, bother," said Pooh, bumping into the walls.

"Pooh?" asked Rabbit.

"How are we ever going
to get him out of there?"
wondered Roo.

Just then, Eeyore arrived
wearing an anchor for his latest tail. Rabbit instructed his friends to
throw the anchor into the pit so Pooh could use it to climb out.

"Whoooaaa!" the friends cried. The heavy anchor yanked them all
down into the hole – and knocked the honeypot off Pooh's head. Now,
they were all stuck.

Only Piglet, who had been tossed high into the air, remained on
the ground.

Now it was up to Piglet to save everyone!

Roo remembered that Christopher Robin owned a jump rope. The friends urged Piglet to go to the boy's house and get it.

A terrified Piglet made his way uncertainly through the Wood – until he saw a red-eyed monster glaring down at him! The little fellow ran and hid. Then the fog cleared, and Piglet realized the monster was only B'loon, stuck in a tree.

Piglet tugged and tugged, trying to free his friend.

Suddenly an enormous shadow fell over him!

Piglet turned and faced the monster. "*B-B-B-BACKSON!*" he shouted. He held on tight to B'loon and ran off.

But there was no Backson – only Tigger dressed in his Backson disguise.

Now Tigger thought the Backson was right behind him, and he ran after his friend for help. "Piglet!" he cried.

"He knows my name!" shrieked Piglet. "Help!"

B'loon lifted Piglet up and away, but it was a very bumpy ride. Then Piglet spotted the pit in the distance. He thought if he could just reach it – and his friends – he would be safe. He had nearly made it when Tigger crashed into him.

Down into the pit they

both tumbled along with an entire paragraph of letters!

When the dust settled, everyone in the pit was
relieved to see that the newcomers were their friends,
and not the Backson.

Just then, B'loon floated up and out
of Piglet's grasp.

"Wait, B'loon!" called Rabbit.
"Don't leave!"

"You have to help us get out
of here!" Piglet cried.

Owl was happy to be stuck a little while longer. Since his friends couldn't go anywhere, they would have to listen to him tell a very, very long story about his uncle.

As Owl talked, a hungry Pooh looked up. He saw the honeypot from Tigger's foot sitting at the edge of the pit – and that's when he decided to use the ladder of letters to climb out.

Unfortunately for Pooh, that honeypot was empty, too. Fortunately for his friends, there was a way out of the pit. Soon they were all back above ground, where Christopher Robin – led by B'loon – joined them.

"How did you escape from the Backson?" wondered Rabbit.

"What on earth is a Backson?" asked Christopher Robin.

"The most wretched creature that you could meet," Owl said solemnly.

"And what gave you the idea I was taken by a Backson?" replied Christopher Robin.

Pooh handed him the note.

Christopher Robin explained that he had written that he would be "back soon" – not "Backson"!

Now that the misunderstanding had been cleared up, Rabbit had an announcement to make. "We owe a very special someone a token of our appreciation," he said. "This reward goes to a good friend who helped us to find Christopher Robin. So I bestow this pot of honey on... B'loon."

"Oh, bother," said Pooh miserably.

The friends went on their way. For Pooh, that meant continuing to search for the honey he and his tummy so desperately wanted.

Eventually, he ended up at Owl's front door where he pulled the bell rope. There was something very familiar about it.

"I found that very handsome bell rope that you were admiring just hanging over a thistle bush," Owl said. "Nobody seemed to want it, so I brought it home." Then he invited Pooh in for some honey.

Pooh suddenly realized that Owl's bell rope was really Eeyore's
tail! Now Owl realized it, too. Pooh left without eating so much as a
drop of honey. Returning Eeyore's tail was far more important.

Soon Eeyore's tail was back where it belonged.
"Seems about the right length. Pink bow's a nice touch. Swishes real
good, too," the donkey decided.

And so Pooh was declared the winner of the tail contest. His friends presented him with the grand prize. It wasn't just a pot of honey, it was an enormous pot of honey.

"Thank you all ever so much," Pooh said. He climbed straight into the pot. All his honey dreams had come true!